This book belongs to

....

Quarto is the authority on a wide range of topics.

Quarto educates, entertains and enriches the lives of our readers—enthusiasts and lovers of hands-on living.

www.quartoknows.com

© 2019 Quarto Publishing plc

First published in 2019 by QEB Publishing, an imprint of The Quarto Group.
6 Orchard Road, Suite 100
Lake Forest, CA 92630
T: +1 949 380 7510
F: +1 949 380 7575
www.QuartoKnows.com

A CIP record for this book is available from the Library of Congress.

ISBN 978-0-7112-4933-2

Based on the original story by Virginie Zurcher and Daniel Howarth
Author of adapted text: Katie Woolley
Series Editor: Joyce Bentley
Series Designer: Sarah Peden

Manufactured in Guangdong, China TT012020
9 8 7 6 5 4 3 2 1

MIX
Paper from responsible sources
FSC® C016973

Reading
Gems

The Star
and the Zoo

QEB

Little Star was high
up in the sky.

Little Star fell down, down, down.

Bump!

Little Star was sad.

All the animals wanted to help.

But Lion could not get Little Star
back in the sky.

But Monkey's plan did not work.

But Giraffe could not get Little Star back in the sky.

Little Star was sad.

Ant wanted to help.

19

Ant's plan did work.

All the ants could help.

Little Star was high up in the sky.

Story Words

Ant

bump

fell

Giraffe

help

Lion

Monkey

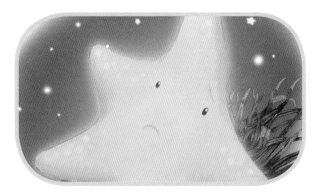

sad

sky

star

zoo

Let's Talk About
The Star and the Zoo

**Look carefully at
the book cover.**

Can you see a star?

What time of day do you
think it is in the story?

What other animals
can you see at the zoo?

**Take a look at the ants
in the picture on page 20.**

How did they get Little Star
back into the sky?

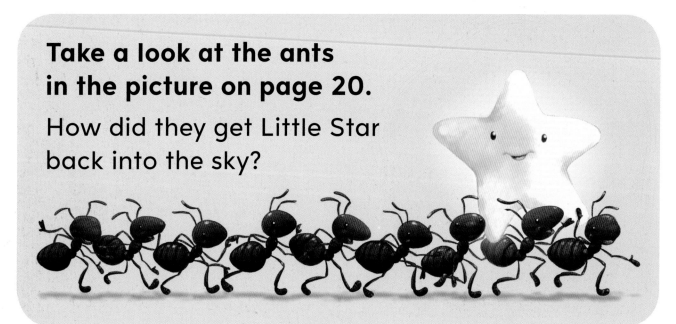

The animals all try to help
Little Star get back in the sky.
How does each animal try to help?
Why does Ant's plan work?

How would you choose to help
Little Star? For example, you
could throw her up in the air
or jump up high on a trampoline.

**Look at the zoo
on pages 4–5
and pages 8–9.**

What different
noises would Little
Star hear at the zoo
in the two pictures?

What noises do
you hear at night?

**Talk about the end
of the story.**

Did you like it?

Do you think the star
is happy or sad now?

27

Fun and Games

Look at these pictures, and find the matching words.

star   monkey   giraffe   ant   lion

Look at these pictures of the characters in this story and their feelings. One picture is different. Which one is it?

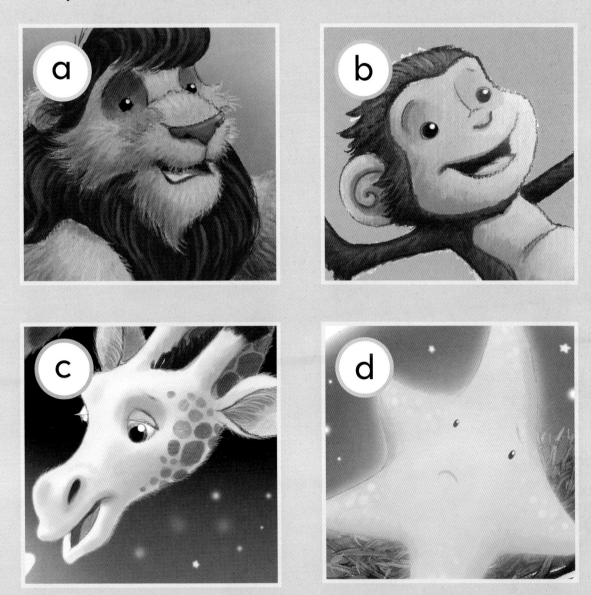

Your Turn

Now that you have read the story,
try telling it in your own words.
Use the pictures below to help you.

READING TOGETHER

- When reading this book together, suggest that your child looks at the pictures to help them make sense of any words they are unsure about, and ask them to point to any letters they recognize.

- Try asking questions such as, "Can you break the word into parts?" and "Are there clues in the picture that help you?"

- During the story, ask your child questions such as, "Can you remember what has happened so far?" and "What do you think will happen next?"

- Look at the story words on pages 24–25 together. Encourage your child to find the pictures and the words on the story pages, too.

- There are lots of activities you can play at home with your child to help them with their reading. Write the alphabet onto 26 cards, and hide them around the house. Encourage your child to shout out the letter name when they find a card!

- In the car, play "I Spy" to help your child learn to recognize the first sound in a word.

- Organize a family read-aloud session once a week! Each family member chooses something to read out loud. It could be their favorite book, a magazine, a menu, or the back of a food package.

- Give your child lots of praise, and take great delight when your child successfully sounds out a new word.

Level 1

Little Star was sad.

Ant wanted to help.

I have a plan.

Short sentences ✓

Simple vocabulary ✓

Lots of repetition ✓

Pictures and words support each other ✓